Christmas decorations & cards

Fiona Watt

Designed by Josephine Thompson
Illustrated by Molly Sage
Photographs by Howard Allman

Contents

There are lots of stickers in the middle of this book. You can use them to decorate the things you make, such as the Christmas collage and the shiny bauble card.

Flying angels

To make an angel's star, like this, press two stickers together, one on each side of the hand.

1. Draw a curved triangle on thick paper for the angel's dress and cut it out. Cut two arms from the same paper, too.

2. Cut out hands and glue them on the arms. Glue one arm behind the dress and glue the other arm on top of the dress.

3. Cut a round head and some hair from paper. Glue the hair onto the head, then glue the head onto the dress.

To make a wing like this angel's, glue gold paper onto the rectangle before you fold it into a zigzag.

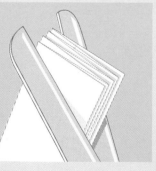

Hold the layers together as you cut.

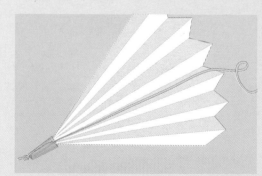

4. Fold a rectangle of paper one way, then the other, to make a zigzag for the wing. Then, cut off the end at an angle.

5. Cut a piece of thread and tie a big knot in one end. Lay the thread in the middle of the zigzag. Then, wrap tape around the end.

6. Hold the wing against the dress, like this. Get someone to help you put a piece of tape across the wing to secure it.

For a sparkly halo, bend a piece of a pipe cleaner into a circle and tape it on.

7. Draw a face on your angel. Then, cut out feet and glue them on the dress. Decorate the angel with paper and stickers.

Hang your angel from a Christmas tree or as a decoration in a window.

Sparkly garland

Decorate your ornaments with stickers from the sticker pages.

1. For a round ornament, draw around a mug on a piece of bright paper. Draw a small shape at the top for hanging.

2. Cut out the ornament. Then, cut a strip of paper and glue it across the middle. Press on stickers or glue on shiny paper.

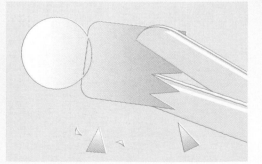

3. For the hanger, draw a rectangle with a circle on top, on shiny paper. Cut it out, then cut a zigzag along the bottom.

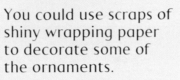

You could use scraps of shiny wrapping paper to decorate some of the ornaments.

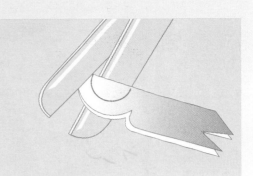

4. Fold the paper and snip a piece out of the middle of the circle to make a hole. Glue the hanger on the top of the ornament.

This tree was decorated with sequins as well as a sticker and glitter.

5. Draw a long, thin ornament. Cut three curved strips and glue them on. Make a hanger for the top and glue it on.

6. Spread stripes of glue across the ornament, then sprinkle it with glitter. Shake off any extra glitter when the glue is dry.

7. Use a hole punch to make a hole at the top of a tree, cut from green paper. Cut a rectangle of paper and glue it on the bottom.

8. Decorate the tree with paper shapes, stickers and sequins. You could also add dots of glitter or glitter glue.

The tape stops the shapes from slipping.

9. Push a piece of ribbon, thread or string through each ornament. Secure them to the ribbon with a tiny piece of tape.

5

Silver trees and birds

Use a glue stick.

1. Cut a large piece of foil from a roll of kitchen foil. Spread glue all over the non-shiny side, then fold the foil in half.

2. Put the folded foil onto an old magazine. Rub the foil so that it sticks together and the surface is smooth.

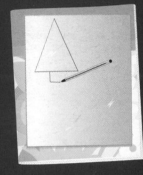

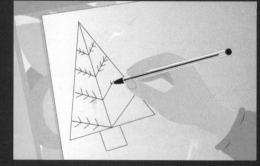

3. For a tree, draw a triangle on the foil with a ballpoint pen. Press hard as you draw. Then, draw a tree trunk at the bottom.

4. Draw a line down the middle of the tree, then add more lines for the branches. Draw lots of little lines on each branch.

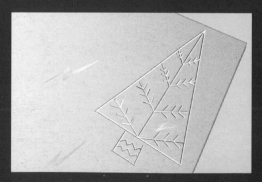

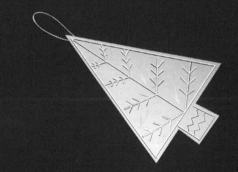

5. Turn the foil over to see the raised lines. Draw more trees, then cut them out, a little way away from their outline.

6. Cut a piece of thread and fold it in half. Tape the ends to the back to make a loop for hanging your decoration.

Birds

1. Draw the outline of a bird's body and beak on the foil. Add wings, an eye and two legs. Don't forget to press hard.

2. Add some lines for the tail, making them end with a curl. Add more curved lines on the head, wings and on the tummy.

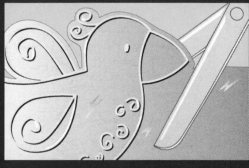

3. Cut around the bird a little way away from the lines you have drawn. Then, tape some thread on the back for hanging.

Christmas collage

 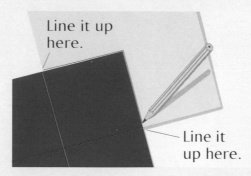 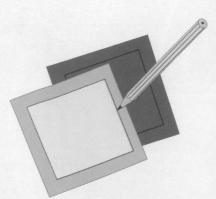

1. Draw a line down the middle of a large piece of thick red paper. Draw two lines across it so that you have six squares.

2. Put a piece of green paper under one corner. Line up the edges with the pencil lines and draw around the corner, like this.

Line it up here.

Line it up here.

3. Cut along the pencil lines to make a square. Then, draw around the square on two different shades of green paper.

4. Cut out the green squares. Glue all the squares on the red paper. Trim the edges if you need to.

5. Decorate each square with a different Christmas picture such as a star, a tree or holly. Cut them from paper or fabric.

6. To make a fan-shaped bird's tail, fold a piece of paper one way then the other to make a zigzag. Glue it at one end only.

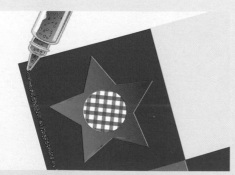 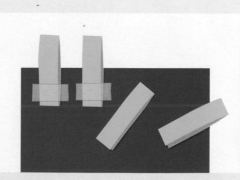 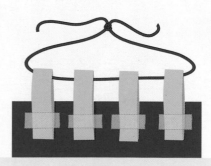

7. Add little details to each picture with glitter, glitter glue and sequins, or glue on pieces of shiny wrapping paper.

8. Turn your collage over, then cut four strips of green paper. Fold each strip in half and tape them along the top.

9. Push a long piece of thread, ribbon or string through each paper loop. Then, tie a double knot in the thread.

Use pieces of shiny wrapping paper.

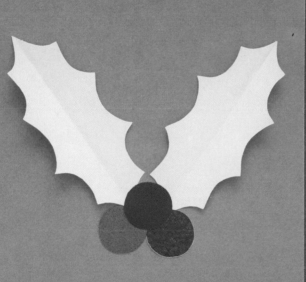

Decorate your collage with stickers from the sticker pages.

If you don't have fabric, use patterned paper from old magazines.

9

Glittering snowflakes

1. Lay an old CD on a piece of thin white paper and draw around it with a pencil. Cut out the circle you have drawn.

2. Fold the paper circle in half, then fold it in half again. Then, fold the shape in half again, so that it looks like this.

CDs often come free with magazines or through the mail to advertise things. You could use one of these.

3. Use scissors to cut a 'V' shape in the tip of the folded circle. Then, cut lots of little triangles around the edges.

4. Gently unfold the paper to see your snowflake. Lay it on a flat surface and smooth it as flat as you can with your fingers.

5. Lay the CD on scrap paper and brush some runny glue around the middle of it. Sprinkle it with glitter and let it dry.

6. Shake any extra glitter off the CD. Then, put lots of little dots of glue on one side of the snowflake and press it on the CD.

7. Let the glue dry, then cut a long piece of thread and tape it to the back. You could then glue another snowflake on top.

These
decorations
were hung
from thick
shiny
thread.

These decorations
look best if you hang
them in a place
where there is
lots of light.

Snowflake baubles

1. Draw around a mug twice on a piece of white paper, then draw around it twice on red paper. Cut out the circles.

2. Cut a strip of thick cardboard about the width of one of the circles. Cut two shorter, narrower strips, too.

3. Pour some red and white paint onto an old plate. Dip the edge of the longest piece of cardboard into the white paint.

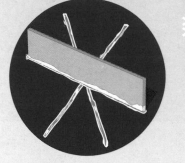

4. Press the edge onto one of the red circles. Print two more lines in an 'X', dipping the cardboard into the paint each time.

5. Use the other pieces of cardboard to print shorter lines on the snowflake. Then, print a snowflake on the other red circle.

Use other edges of the cardboard for the red paint.

6. Print red snowflakes in the same way on the white circles, then leave them until the paint is completely dry.

7. Fold each circle in half, along one of the long printed lines. Then, spread glue on one half of one of the red circles.

For a sparkly
snowflake, like
the one at the top,
print the lines with glue
and sprinkle them with glitter.

8. Press one half of a white circle onto the glue, matching the edge and the fold. Then, spread glue on its other half.

9. Press on the other red circle, matching the edge and fold as before. Then, make a loop in a piece of thread and tape it inside.

10. Glue one half of one of the red circles and press on the remaining white circle. Then, glue the last two halves together.

Pipe cleaner trees

The star on this tree was cut out from holographic paper.

Fold the paper in half, like this.

1. Cut a piece of wrapping paper just over the height of this page and half its width. Fold it in half, with the pattern on the inside.

2. Find the middle of the fold by bending it in half, but not actually creasing it. Then, pinch the fold to mark the middle.

Keep the paper folded as you cut.

3. Draw a line from the middle mark to each corner. Then, cut along the lines to make two triangular trees.

4. Bend the end of a pipe cleaner around to make a loop. Then, cut across the top of the trees to make two small triangles.

Shiny wrapping paper with simple patterns, like these stars, works well.

You could hang these decorations on a Christmas tree or on some branches.

5. Spread glue on one of the triangles, then lay the pipe cleaner on top. Glue the other one and press it on, matching the edges.

Leave a small gap.

6. Hold the trees together and cut across again to make two strips. Glue the strips on either side of the pipe cleaner.

7. Continue cutting strips across the trees and gluing them on until they are almost at the bottom of the pipe cleaner.

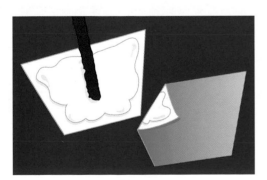

8. Cut out a pot from some folded wrapping paper and glue the pieces on. Add star stickers on either side of the top of the tree.

Use stickers from the sticker pages and glitter to decorate plain paper.

Simple snowflakes

Use a ballpoint pen.

Curl this end around for hanging.

1. Cut a piece of cellophane from some packaging. Put a saucer on top and draw around it. Cut out the circle.

2. Cut a piece of string wider than the circle. Paint it with household glue (PVA) and press it on the cellophane, like this.

For silver string, mix the glue with silver paint.

3. Cut two more pieces of string about the width of the circle. Paint them with glue. Lay them over the first one in an 'X' shape.

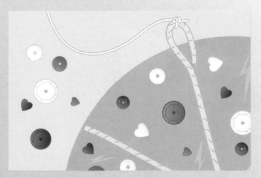

Use stickers from the sticker pages to decorate the snowflakes.

4. When the glue is dry, decorate the snowflake with sequins or stickers. Tie some thread around the loop for hanging.

Robin decorations

1. Cut a strip of white paper about the height of this book. Bend it around to make an oval and glue it together, like this.

2. For the eye, cut a short strip of white paper. Roll it around a pencil and glue the end. Glue it inside the body.

You could hang these decorations in a window or on a Christmas tree.

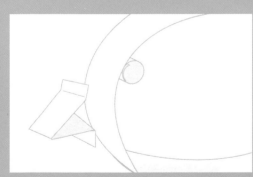

3. Cut a strip of paper for the beak. Fold it in half, then bend a little bit back at each end. Glue the ends onto the body.

4. Then, cut a strip of red paper. Bend it into a teardrop shape and glue the ends. Glue it inside for the bird's tummy.

5. Glue on a strip for a tail. Make two small cuts in it, then curl the end around a pencil. Tape on some thread for hanging.

Bouncing snowman

To make your snowman bounce, pull one of its boots gently, then let go.

This snowman's scarf was made from strips of paper.

Glue buttons, cut from paper, on the snowman's body.

18

1. For the body, draw around a large plate on a piece of thin white paper. Cut out the circle you have drawn and fold it in half.

2. Draw a line from the fold of the circle almost to the edge. Then, draw one from the edge almost to the fold, like this.

Make the lines about two finger widths apart.

3. Then, draw another line coming from the fold almost to the edge. Make this two finger widths below the second line.

4. Continue to draw lines from the fold, then from the edge. Then, cut along the pencil lines, keeping the paper folded.

5. Unfold the circle and flatten it. Then, draw around a saucer for the head. Cut it out and glue it onto the body.

6. Cut a hat from a piece of black paper and glue it on. Draw on eyes and a mouth with felt-tip pens, and glue on a paper nose.

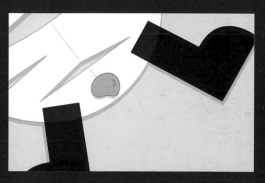

7. Cut out arms, like sticks, from black paper and glue them on the back of the body. Cut out boots and glue them on, too.

8. Cut a piece of thread or ribbon and tape it to the back of the hat. Hold the snowman's hat and gently pull the body to stretch it.

9. Before you hang your snowman press some poster tack onto the bottom of the body. This will help it bounce.

Spots and stars card

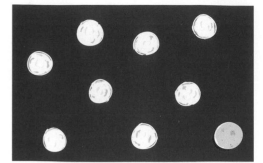

1. Cut two small potatoes in half. Then, use an old spoon to spread a patch of white paint onto a pile of kitchen paper towels.

2. Dip the cut side of one of the potatoes into the paint. Press it onto a large piece of red paper, then lift it off.

3. Dip the potato into the paint again and do another print. Do this lots of times until the paper is covered in white spots.

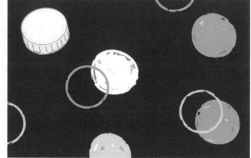

Use a different potato for each paint.

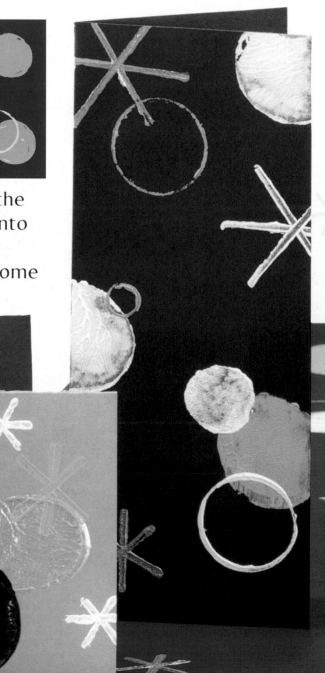

4. Spread some silver and blue paint onto the paper towels and print lots more spots. Make some of them overlap the white ones.

5. For the circles, dip the edge of a bottle top into one of the paints and print it, overlapping some of the spots.

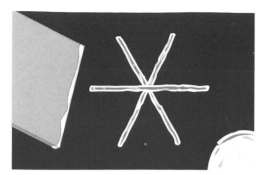

Instead of making cards, use the whole sheet of paper as wrapping paper.

6. For the stars, dip the edge of a piece of cardboard into some paint and print a line. Print two more lines in an 'X' on top.

7. Leave the paint to dry, then cut the paper into several rectangles. Fold each rectangle in half to make a card.

You could cut out a circle as a gift tag and attach it to a present with ribbon.

Shiny bauble card

1. For a long card, fold a rectangle of thick paper in half, with its long sides together, and crease the fold well.

Use stickers from the sticker pages to decorate some of the baubles.

The strings on these cards were drawn with gold and silver pens.

Use shiny paper if you have it.

 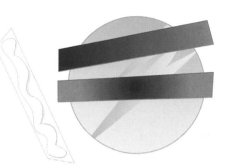 

2. Draw around several small jar lids on the back of pieces of wrapping paper. Cut out the circles you have drawn.

3. For a striped bauble, cut strips of shiny paper. Glue them across one of the circles, letting the strips overlap the edges.

4. When the glue is dry, turn the bauble over. Then, cut off the ends of the strips which overlap the edge of the circle.

5. To make a bauble with stars, press stickers onto one of your shiny circles. Make some of them overlap the edges.

6. Trim off all the extra pieces of the stickers which are overlapping the edges of the circle, as you did before.

7. Decorate the other shiny circles with different patterns of stripes, stars and circles. Use stickers or cut shapes from paper.

8. Glue the circles onto the card at different levels. Use a felt-tip pen to draw a string from the top of the card to each bauble.

Zigzag card

To make the card stand up, pull the front layer forward to make a zigzag.

1. Cut a long, thin rectangle of thick paper or very thin cardboard. Fold it in half lengthways and crease the fold well.

Middle fold

2. Fold the top layer over until it meets the middle fold. Turn the card over and fold it in the same way, to make a zigzag.

3. Open the card and draw a wavy line from one side of the card to the other, like this. Use a pencil and press lightly.

4. Cut along the line you have drawn but stop at the last fold. Then, cut down the fold from the top, as far as the pencil line.

The shapes are shown in yellow here so you can see them.

5. Fold the card into a zigzag again. Then, use a white wax crayon to draw some stars and a moon. Press hard as you draw.

6. Open the card, then paint over the stars and moon with blue paint as far as the pencil line. The shapes will resist the paint.

7. While the sky is drying, draw lots of dots on some thick paper with the white wax crayon. Then, paint green paint over the top.

If you want to draw lines on the trees, like those on two of these cards, cut out the triangles before you draw them at step 7.

Overlap the little trees.

8. When the paint is dry, cut out about eight little triangles for the trees. Make them slightly different sizes.

9. Glue three of the trees onto the back layer of the card. Then, glue another one on the layer in front, like this.

10. Lay the rest of the trees on the top two layers so that they don't overlap any of the other trees. Then, glue them on.

Sparkling card

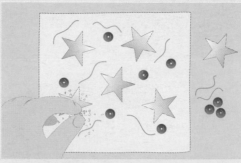

1. Cut two squares of clear book covering film. Make them the same size. Then, peel the backing paper off one of them.

These cards really sparkle if you sprinkle lots of glitter over the film.

2. Lay the film on a table, sticky-side up. Press lots of sequins and little pieces of thread onto the film. Then, sprinkle on some glitter.

3. Peel the backing paper off the other piece of film and lay it, sticky-side down, on the decorated piece of film.

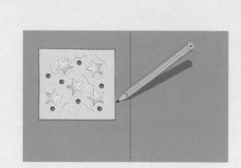

4. Fold a piece of thick paper in half. Open it out again and draw around the film, on the left-hand side, like this.

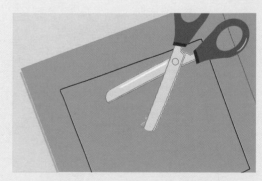

5. Push a sharp pencil into the middle of the shape to make a hole. Then, push the blade of some scissors into the hole.

6. Cut a 'window' in the paper, smaller than the shape you drew. Don't worry if the sides don't make a perfect square.

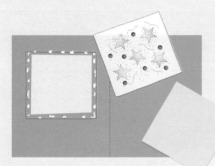

Here are some ideas of different shapes of 'windows' cut into some cards.

7. Glue around the 'window', then press on the decorated film. Then, cut a square of paper and glue it over the film.

You could use this technique to make gift tags too.

Printed reindeer

1. Cut a potato in half, lengthways. Then, turn it over and cut away two pieces at the sides, to make a handle.

2. Lay a few kitchen paper towels in a pile on a newspaper. Pour brown paint on top and spread it out with an old spoon.

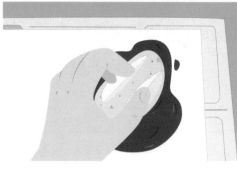

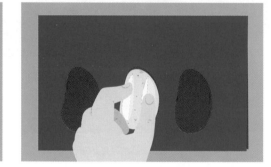

3. Holding the handle, press the flat side of the potato firmly onto the patch of brown paint, then lift it up.

4. Press the potato onto some paper to print the reindeer's head. Press the potato into the paint again and do more prints.

5. For the reindeer's ears, dip your middle finger into the brown paint. Fingerprint an ear on either side of the head.

6. When the brown paint is dry, pour red paint onto the paper towels and spread it out. Dip your first finger into the paint.

7. Fingerprint a red nose near the bottom of each head. Then, use a black felt-tip pen to draw two eyes on each one.

8. When the paint is dry, draw two long lines for antlers. Then, draw a few smaller lines on each side of the long lines.

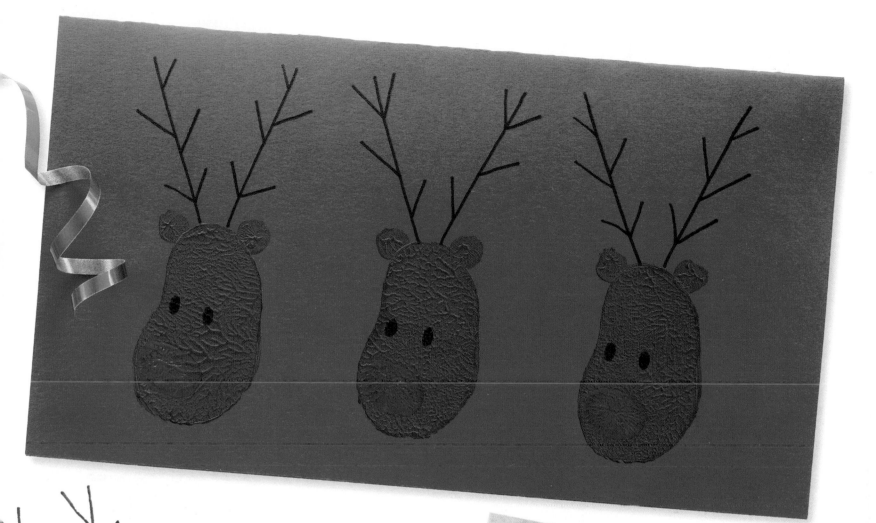

You could print the
reindeer on a card or
gift tag, or just do
them on paper for fun.

Snowman card

Press star stickers in the sky around the snowman.

You could add stick arms with a felt-tip pen.

Cut a hat from black paper and glue it on.

1. Cut a rectangle from blue paper. Then, cut a piece of thick white paper exactly the same size. Fold both of them in half.

2. Open the blue paper. Draw a wavy line across one side of the card for snow. Draw the outline of a snowman on the line.

3. Use scissors to cut along the line for the snow, then around the snowman and along the line for snow again.

4. Spread glue over the bottom half of the blue card. Then, press one side of the white card onto it, matching the edges.

5. Spread glue over the top of the blue card, around the snowman. Then, close the card, pressing it down onto the white card.

This card had two snowman shapes drawn on the wavy line (see step 2).

6. Draw eyes and a line of dots for the mouth. Add a nose and a hat and press on stickers for buttons.

Santa card

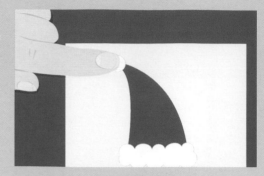

1. Fold a square of thick paper in half to make a card. Cut a curved hat from red paper and glue it near the top.

2. Cut a beard with a wavy outline from white paper. Glue it on the card below the hat, leaving a gap between the two.

3. Cut a wavy strip from white paper and glue it on the hat. Press on a white sticker too, or cut one from paper.

Try cutting out different shapes of Santa hats.

4. Cut out a nose from red paper and glue it on. Press on two stickers for eyes. Then, add a smile with a red felt-tip pen.

Photographic manipulation: Emma Julings • With thanks to Rachel Bright

First published in 2003 by Usborne Publishing Ltd., 83-85 Saffron Hill, London, EC1N 8RT www.usborne.com

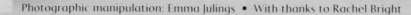